"I can't," she said, knowing how inadequate it sounded but unable to explain. How could she ever say everything she would need to say in order to make him understand? "I can't."

"Because I am Monterossan, of course."

Her throat was tight. "No, not because of that."

He raked a hand through his hair. She could still see the firm ridge of his arousal beneath his shorts. "Then why, Antonella? I know when a woman wants me. And you do. As much as I want you, God help me."

God help me.

Her heart ached as she hopped off the vanity and tugged her dress back down. "Maybe that is why, Cristiano."

"Because you want me you will deny me?" Fury took the place of resignation.

"No, not because of that. Because you despise me—and you despise yourself for wanting me anyway."

All about the author...
Lynn Raye Harris

LYNN RAYE HARRIS read her first Harlequin romance when her grandmother carted home a box from a yard sale. She didn't know she wanted to be a writer then, but she definitely knew she wanted to marry a sheikh or a prince and live the glamorous life she read about in the pages. Instead, she married a military man and moved around the world. She's been inside the Kremlin, hiked up a Korean mountain, floated on a gondola in Venice and stood inside volcanoes at opposite ends of the world.

These days Lynn lives in north Alabama with her handsome husband and two crazy cats. When she's not writing, she loves to read, shop for antiques, cook gourmet meals and try new wines. She is also an avowed shoeaholic and thinks there's nothing better than a new pair of high heels.

Lynn was a finalist in the 2008 Romance Writers of America's Golden Heart contest, and she is the winner of the Harlequin Presents® Instant Seduction contest. She loves a hot hero, a heroine with attitude, and a happy ending. Writing passionate stories for Harlequin Books is a dream come true. You can visit her at www.lynnrayeharris.com.

FLORA SPEER

Rose Red

A Faerie Tale Romance

Once upon a time...they lived happily ever after.

"I HAVE TWO DAUGHTERS, ONE A FLOWER AS PURE AND WHITE AS THE NEW-FALLEN SNOW AND THE OTHER A ROSE AS RED AND SWEET AS THE FIRES OF PASSION."

Bianca and Rosalinda are the only treasures left to their mother after her husband, the Duke of Monteferro, is murdered. Fleeing a remote villa in the shadows of the Alps of Northern Italy, she raises her daughters in hiding and swears revenge on the enemy who has brought her low.

The years pass until one stormy night a stranger appears from out of the swirling snow, half-frozen and wild, wrapped only in a bearskin. To gentle Bianca he appears a gallant suitor. To their mother he is the son of an assassin. But to Rosalinda he is the one man who can light the fires of passion and make them burn as sweet and red as her namesake.

_52139-3 $5.99 US/$6.99 CAN

Rejar

DARA JOY

Lord Byron thinks he's a scream, the fashionable matrons titter behind their fans at a glimpse of his hard form, and nobody knows where he came from. His startling eyes—one gold, one blue—promise a wicked passion, and his voice almost seems to purr. There is only one thing a woman thinks of when looking at a man like that. *Sex.* And there is only one woman he seems to want. *Lilac.* In her wildest dreams she never guesses that bringing a stray cat into her home will soon have her stroking the most wanted man in 1811 London....

_52178-4 $5.99 US/$6.99 CAN

DEBRA DIER
LORD SAVAGE
Author of *Scoundrel*

Lady Elizabeth Barrington is sent to Colorado to find the Marquess of Angelstone, the grandson of an English duke who disappeared during an attack by renegade Indians. But the only thing she discovers is Ash MacGregor, a bounty-hunting rogue who takes great pleasure residing in the back of a bawdy house. Convinced that his rugged good looks resemble those of the noble family, Elizabeth vows she will prove to him that aristocratic blood does pulse through his veins. And in six month's time, she will make him into a proper man. But the more she tries to show him which fork to use or how to help a lady into her carriage, the more she yearns to be caressed by this virile stranger, touched by this beautiful barbarian, embraced by Lord Savage.

_4119-7 $4.99 US/$5.99 CAN